Ninja Nate

By Markette Sheppard
Illustrated by Robert Paul Jr.

A Denene Millner Book
Simon & Schuster Books for Young Readers
New York London Toronto Sydney New Delhi

Nathaniel Brown
is a ten-year-old ninja master.
Or so he thinks.

All summer long,

Nathaniel has been dressing up like one.

He **eats,**

plays,

and **sleeps** in his ninja suit.

Nathaniel dresses up like a ninja so much that his friends started calling him **"Ninja Nate."**

But he's **not really** a ninja. Ninja Nate is actually an almost-fifth grader. And while he's a master at play-jitsu, Ninja Nate is just **like any other kid.**

Ninja Nate's **sensei** is his big brother, Charlie. Charlie does not think he's a sensei, although he does think Ninja Nate got **all his moves** from him.

That's why Charlie prefers
to call himself **a boss.**

Of course, the real boss is Ninja Nate's mom, Mary. Mama Mary makes sure that kid ninjas get their proper care between snack-time rumbles and playtime fumbles.

BOSS
MAMA

But it's up to Ninja Nate to keep up
with his silver sword.

He thinks his sword would be better
if it were sharper and decorated with magical gems
that could do stuff, like turn back time
and heal things that break.

It's still a **pretty awesome** sword, though. It has helped Ninja Nate through some of his **biggest battles** of the summer.

SUGAR PUFFS
MUNDANE BITES
DULLY BEAR
BLAND'S EXTRA
LACK LUSTER CLUSTERS
BLAND'S

The night before the **first day of school,** Ninja Nate dreamt of a land of a gazillion **nefarious ninjas.**

They were all marching toward **Ninja Nate,**

determined to devour

Potato Chip Dip Mountain.

Battle after battle, all throughout the night,
Ninja Nate fended them off the snack-filled peak.
Just when he was about to go against the **biggest**
ninja of them all . . .

THUMP!

He fell out of his bed.

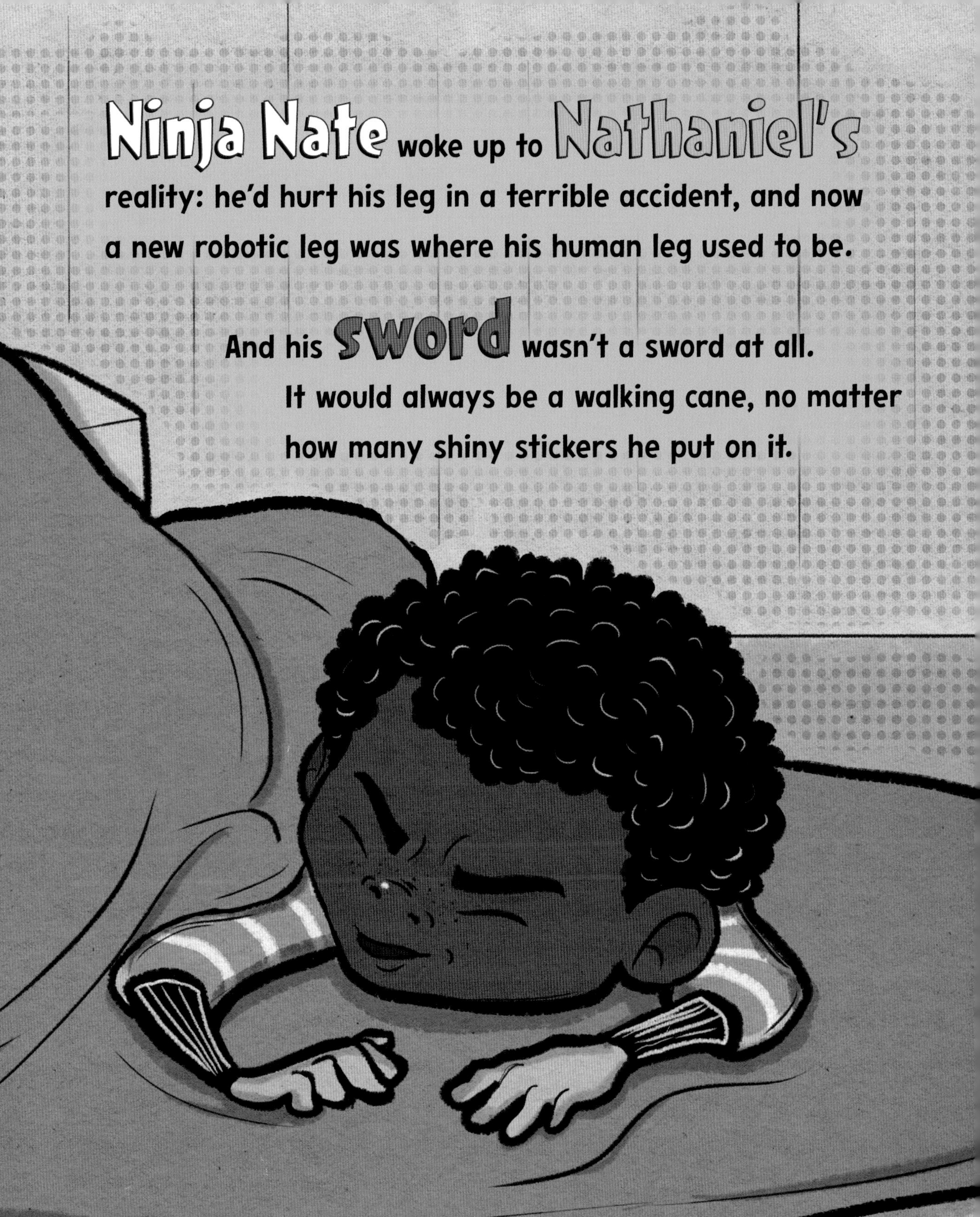

Ninja Nate woke up to Nathaniel's reality: he'd hurt his leg in a terrible accident, and now a new robotic leg was where his human leg used to be.

And his sword wasn't a sword at all. It would always be a walking cane, no matter how many shiny stickers he put on it.

"Charlieeeeeee!"

Nathaniel called out.

"Yo! You really gotta start keeping this thing next to your bed," said Charlie in a sensei kind of way. "Let me help you up."

As much as Ninja Nate had hoped his dream
was reality and his reality was a dream,
the truth was he was simply Nathaniel,
hiding his robotic leg under his ninja costume.

His robotic leg came in his favorite colors, but he was worried about what the other kids would think about the "new" him. That made him a little sad and a little scared.

"It's going to be all right," Mama Mary encouraged. "One step at a time."

After all that worry, the first day of school wasn't so bad.

On the playground, Nathaniel rocked as Ninja Nate—part boy, part robot, all ninja!

Everybody loved his **cool ninja moves.**

He also rocked as, simply, Nathaniel.
Everybody loved that he was smart and kind.

Some of the kids knew that **Ninja Nate** was a little different from Nathaniel Brown, but they didn't care.

And soon enough, there wasn't even a difference at all.

To Wesley, a skilled artist and lover of martial arts whose most impressive jutsu is his kindhearted nature. Thank you for teaching me as much about life as I teach you.
–M.S.

To my mother,
the original "Boss Mama."
–R.P.Jr.

SIMON & SCHUSTER BOOKS FOR YOUNG READERS • An imprint of Simon & Schuster Children's Publishing Division • 1230 Avenue of the Americas, New York, New York 10020 • Text © 2023 by Markette Sheppard • Illustration © 2023 by Robert Paul Jr. • Book design by Sarah Creech © 2023 by Simon & Schuster, Inc. • For information about special discounts for bulk purchases, please contact Simon & Schuster Special Sales at 1-866-506-1949 or business@simonandschuster.com. • The Simon & Schuster Speakers Bureau can bring authors to your live event. For more information or to book an event, contact the Simon & Schuster Speakers Bureau at 1-866-248-3049 or visit our website at www.simonspeakers.com. • The text for this book was set in Comicraft Hero Sandwich Pro and Monotype Dreamland. • The illustrations were rendered digitally with scanned, cold-pressed watercolor paper, chalk, and dry pastels. • Manufactured in China • 0523 SCP • First Edition • 2 4 6 8 10 9 7 5 3 1 • CIP data for this book is available from the Library of Congress. • ISBN 9781534476929 • ISBN 9781534476936 (ebook)